SCUFFY
THE TUGBOAT

and His Adventures Down the River

By Gertrude Crampton

WITH PICTURES BY TIBOR GERGELY

A GOLDEN BOOK • NEW YORK
Western Publishing Company, Inc., Racine, Wisconsin 53404

A GOLDEN BOOK • NEW YORK

Copyright © 1946, 1955, renewed 1974, 1983 by Random House, Inc. All rights reserved. Published in the United States by Golden Books, an imprint of Random House Children's Books, a division of Random House, Inc., New York. GOLDEN BOOKS, A GOLDEN BOOK, A LITTLE GOLDEN BOOK, the G colophon, and the distinctive gold spine are registered trademarks of Random House, Inc. Scuffy the Tugboat is a registered trademark of Random House, Inc.
www.goldenbooks.com
Educators and librarians, for a variety of teaching tools, visit us at
www.randomhouse.com/kids
www.randomhouse.com/teachers
Library of Congress Control Number: 2002100498
ISBN: 0-307-02046-0
PRINTED IN CHINA

Scuffy was sad.

Scuffy was cross.

Scuffy sniffed his blue smokestack.

"A toy store is no place for a red-painted tug-boat," said Scuffy, and he sniffed his blue smokestack again. "I was meant for bigger things."

"Perhaps you would not be cross if you went sailing," said the man with the polka dot tie, who owned the shop.

So one night he took Scuffy home to his little boy. He filled the bathtub with water.

"Sail, little tugboat," said the little boy.

"I won't sail in a bathtub," said Scuffy. "A tub is no place for a red-painted tugboat. I was meant for bigger things."

The next day the man with the polka dot tie and his little boy carried Scuffy to a laughing brook that started high in the hills.

"Sail, little tugboat," said the man with the polka dot tie.

It was Spring, and the brook was full to the brim with its water. And the water moved in a hurry, as all things move in a hurry when it is Spring.

Scuffy was in a hurry, too.

"Come back little tugboat, come back," cried the little boy as the hurrying, brimful brook carried Scuffy downstream.

"Not I," tooted Scuffy. "Not I. This is the life for me."

All that day Scuffy sailed along with the brook.
Past the meadows filled with cowslips. Past the
women washing clothes on the bank. Past the
little woods filled with violets.

Cows came to the brook to drink.

They stood in the cool water, and it was fun

to sail around between their legs and bump softly
into their noses.

It was fun to see them drink.

But when a white and brown cow almost drank
Scuffy instead of the brook's cool water, Scuffy was
frightened. That was not fun!

Night came, and with it the moon.

There was nothing to see but the quiet trees.

Suddenly an owl called out, "Hoot! Hooot!"

"Toot, tooot!" cried the frightened tugboat, and he wished he could see the smiling face of the man with the polka dot tie.

When morning came, Scuffy was cross instead of frightened.

"I was meant for bigger things, but which way am I to go?" he said. But there was only one way to go, and that was with the running water where the two brooks met to form a small river. And with the river sailed Scuffy, the red-painted tugboat.

He was proud when he sailed past villages.
"People build villages at the edge of my river,"
said Scuffy, and he straightened his blue smokestack.

Once Scuffy's river joined a small one jammed with logs. Here were men in heavy jackets and great boots, walking about on the floating logs, trying to pry them free.

"Toot, toot, let me through," demanded Scuffy. But the men paid no attention to him. They pushed the logs apart so they would drift with the river to the sawmill in the town. Scuffy bumped along with the jostling logs.

"Ouch!" he cried as two logs bumped together.

"This is a fine river," said Scuffy, "but it's very busy and very big for me."

He was proud when he sailed under the bridges.

"My river is so wide and so deep that people must build bridges to cross it."

The river moved through big towns now instead of villages.

And the bridges over it were very wide—wide enough so that many cars and trucks and streetcars could cross all at once.

The river got deeper and deeper. Scuffy did not have to tuck up his bottom.

The river moved faster and faster.

"I feel like a train instead of a tugboat," said Scuffy, as he was hurried along.

He was proud when he passed the old saw mill with its water wheel.

But high in the hills and mountains the winter snow melted. Water filled the brooks and rushed from there into the small rivers. Faster and faster it flowed, to the great river where Scuffy sailed.

"There is too much water in this river," said Scuffy, as he pitched and tossed on the waves. "Soon it will splash over the top and what a flood there will be!"

Soon great armies of men came to save the fields and towns from the rushing water.

They filled bags with sand and put them at the edge of the river.

"They're making higher banks for the river," shouted Scuffy, "to hold the water back." The water rose higher and higher.

The men built the sand bags higher and higher. Higher! went the river. Higher! went the sand bags.

At last the water rose no more. The flood water rushed on to the sea, and Scuffy raced along with the flood. The people and the fields and the towns were safe.

On went the river to the sea. At last Scuffy
sailed into a big city. Here the river widened, and
all about were docks and wharves.

Oh, it was a busy place and a noisy place! The cranes groaned as they swung the cargoes into great ships. The porters shouted as they carried suitcases and boxes on board.

Horses stamped and truck motors roared, streetcars clanged and people shouted. Scuffy said, "Toot, toot," but nobody noticed.

"Oh, oh!" cried Scuffy when he saw the sea. "There is no beginning and there is no end to the sea. I wish I could find the man with the polka dot tie and his little boy!"

Just as the little red-painted tugboat sailed past the last piece of land, a hand reached out and picked him up. And there was the man with the polka dot tie, with his little boy beside him.

Scuffy is home now with the man with the polka dot tie and his little boy.

He sails from one end of the bathtub to the other.

"This is the place for a red-painted tugboat," says Scuffy. "And this is the life for me."